# twilight

## THE GRAPHIC NOVEL ♦ VOLUME 1

# STEPHENIE MEYER

### ART AND ADAPTATION BY YOUNG KIM

atom

www.atombooks.co.uk

ATOM

First published in Great Britain in 2010 by Atom

Art and Adaptation: Young Kim

Text copyright © 2005 by Stephenie Meyer
Illustrations © 2010 Hachette Book Group, Inc.

The moral right of the author has been asserted.

*All characters and events in this publication, other than
those clearly in the public domain, are fictitious
and any resemblance to real persons,
living or dead, is purely coincidental.*

A CIP catalogue record for this book
is available from the British Library.

ISBN 978-1-905654-66-6

Printed and bound in Italy

Atom
An imprint of
Little, Brown Book Group
100 Victoria Embankment
London EC4Y 0DY

An Hachette UK Company
www.hachette.co.uk

www.atombooks.co.uk

*I love* Twilight: The Graphic Novel.

*It's simply beautiful.*

*Working with Young was always very exciting,*

*but more than that,*

*it brought me back to my first* Twilight *experience.*

*She would send me a new set of drawings,*

*some portrait of Edward or Bella would jump off the page*

*and suddenly I would be feeling all the same things I felt*

*that first summer while I was writing their story.*

*The art made it fresh again.*

*I hope everyone has that same experience with it.*

— *Stephenie Meyer*

⤙ ⤚

*I'd never given much thought to how I would die —*

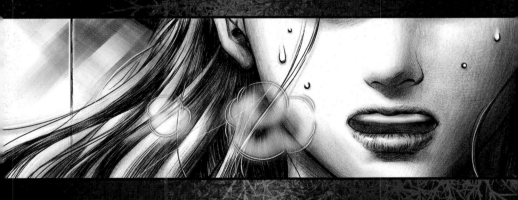

*— though I'd had reason enough
in the last few months...*

*Surely it was a good way to die...*

...in the place of someone else, someone I loved.

The hunter smiled in a friendly way...

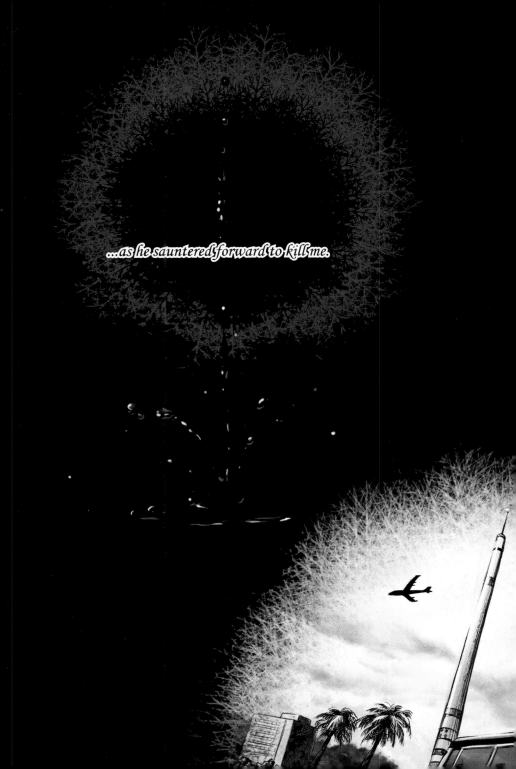

...as he sauntered forward to kill me.

*I exiled myself to the tiny town of Forks,*
*in the Olympic Peninsula of northwest Washington State,*
*where my dad, Charlie, lived...*

...trading Phoenix, the hot, sunny, sprawling city that I loved, for gloomy Forks and its near-constant cover of clouds...

To my intense surprise, I loved my new — well, new to me — truck.

It took only one trip to get all my stuff upstairs. Everything in the room was a part of my childhood...even the rocking chair from my baby days was there.

One of the best things about Charlie is he doesn't hover. So I didn't have to smile and look pleased.

*I didn't relate well to people my age.*

*...Maybe the truth was that I didn't relate well to people, period.*

*So what were my chances here?*

splat

splat

I was the new girl at Forks High School, which had a frightening total of only three hundred and fifty-seven students.

I have your schedule right here, and a map of the school.

Thanks.

*Hopefully, I won't have to walk around with this map stuck in front of my nose all day.*

There was always someone braver than the others who would introduce themselves.

You're Isabella Swan, aren't you?

Bella.

Where's your next class?

I could show you the way to your building. Oh, I'm Eric.

*He's definitely the over-helpful type...*

Getting into
the cafeteria,
trying to make
conversation with
several
curious
strangers...

It was there...

*...that I first saw them.*

*Every one of them was chalky pale...*

*They all had very dark eyes despite the range in hair tones...*

They also had dark shadows under those eyes.

But all this is not why I couldn't look away.

I stared because their faces were inhumanly beautiful, just like on the airbrushed pages of a fashion magazine...

*...or the face of an angel, painted by an old master...*

Who are *they?*

Is he...
staring at
me?

His tight fist never loosened.

What was wrong with him? Was this his normal behavior?

It couldn't... have anything to do with me.

*The next day was better...*

...and worse.

FORKS HIGH SCHOOL

NO SMOKING

200

*I dreaded his bizarre glares...*

*...but part of me wanted to confront him and demand to know what his problem was.*

But...

*...Edward Cullen wasn't in school at all.*

together the way a family should — camping trips every other weekend...

Just because they're newcomers, people have to talk.

*Edward Cullen didn't come back to school the rest of the week.*

So, in two weeks...

Ridiculous.
I shouldn't have to run away.

Bella —!!

Please, Bella.
Trust me.

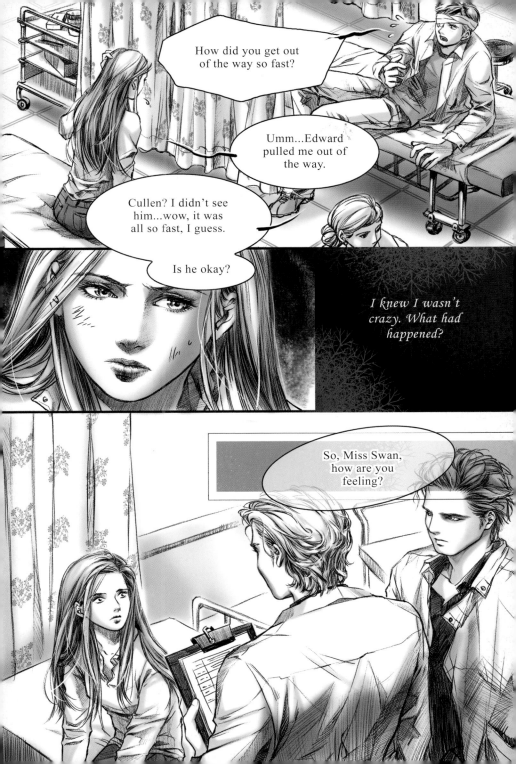

I don't know.

*That was the first night
I dreamed of Edward Cullen.*

After that...he was in my dreams nearly
every night, but always on the periphery,
never within reach.

And the month that followed
the accident was uneasy.
To my dismay, I found myself
the center of attention.

...Edward seemed totally unaware of my presence. I watched as his golden eyes grew perceptibly darker day by day.

He wished he hadn't pulled me from the path of Tyler's van — there was no other conclusion I could come to.

......?

Bella?

*It was the first time he'd looked at me in six weeks.*

What? Are you speaking to me again?

You don't know anything.

"It's better if we're not friends."

I'd been to the beaches around La Push many times, so First Beach was familiar to me. It was still breathtaking.

Some of the boys wanted to hike to the nearby tidal pools. I got up quietly to join the group. When we got back to First Beach, the group we'd left behind had multiplied.

They were teenagers from the reservation who had come to socialize.

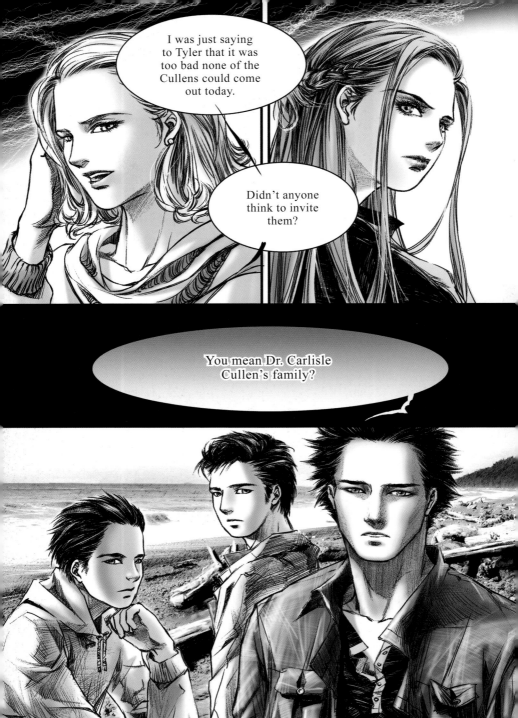

The Cullens don't come here.

*What does he mean?*

So...is Forks driving you insane yet?

Oh, that's an under-statement.

...Do you want to walk down the beach with me?

Oops. I'm not supposed to say anything about that.

Oh, I won't tell anyone, I'm just curious.

......

...Do you like scary stories?

Do you know any of our old stories, about where we came from — the Quileutes, I mean?

Not really.

They are the *same* ones.

WOOOOSHHHH·····

WOOOOSHHHH·····

*The sound of waves crashing against the rocks somewhere nearby.*

CREAK....

*I couldn't avoid it anymore.*

Throughout the vast shadowy world of ghosts and demons there is no figure so terrible, no figure so dreaded and abhorred, yet dight with such fearful fascination, as the vampire, who is himself neither ghost nor demon, but yet who partakes the dark natures and possesses the mysterious and terrible qualities of both.

—Rev. Montague Summers

*click*

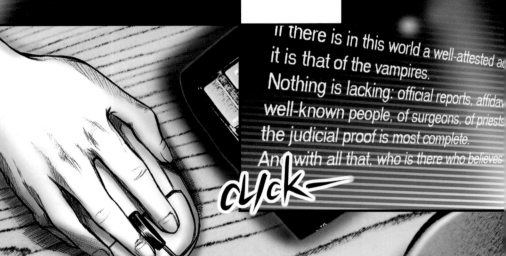

If there is in this world a well-attested ac
it is that of the vampires.
Nothing is lacking: official reports, affidav
well-known people, of surgeons, of priests
the judicial proof is most complete.
And with all that, who is there who believes

*click*

## The Myths of Vampires

| Filipino Danag | Hebrew Estrie | Polish Upier | |
|---|---|---|---|
| | | | |

*click*

Romanian
Varacolaci

A powerful undead being who could appear as a beautiful, pale-skinned hum...

*click*

Slovakian
Nelapsi

A creature so strong and fast it could massacre an entire village in the single hour after midnight

*click*

Italian
Stregoni benefici

An Italian Vampire,
said to be on the side of goodness,
and a mortal enemy of all evil vampires.

*There was little that coincided
with Jacob's stories or my own
observations.*

I forced myself to focus on the two most vital questions I had to answer.

First, I had to decide if it was possible that what Jacob had said about the Cullens could be true...Could the Cullens be vampires?

Whether it be Jacob's cold ones or my own superhero theory, Edward Cullen was not...human.

So then—maybe. That would have to be my answer for now.

And then the most important question of all.

What was I going to do
if it was true?

Avoid him as much
as possible?

A sudden agony of
despair gripped me
as I considered that
alternative.

There was one thing I was sure
of, if I was sure of anything.

In my dream, it
wasn't fear for the
wolf that brought
the cry of "no" to
my lips.

It was fear that he
would be harmed.

I knew in that I had my answer.

I didn't know if there ever was a choice, really. I was already in too deep.

I wanted nothing more than to be with him right now.

The decision was made. Once I realized it, I felt more serene than I'd ever felt.

I was painfully eager to see not just him but all the Cullens — but there was no sign of Edward or any of his family all day.

The good mood brought on by the sunshine vanished.

...The next day was sunny again, but the silver Volvo was still nowhere to be found.

Bella, Angela and I are going dress shopping for the dance. Come with us!

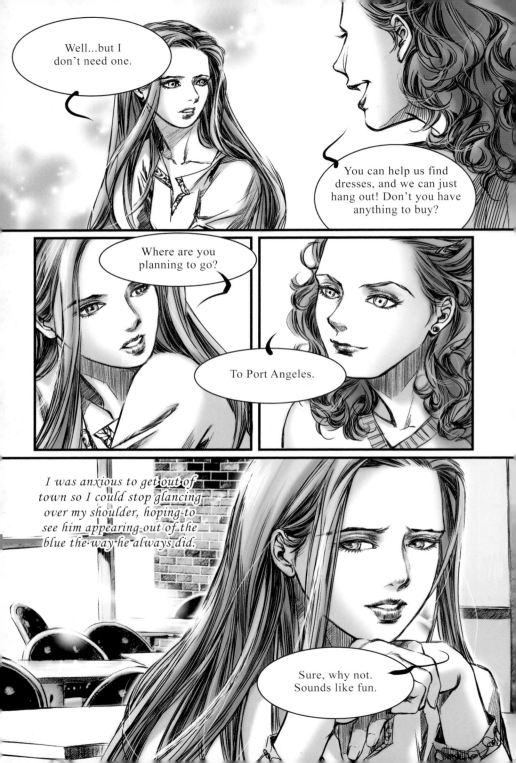

The dress shopping didn't take as long as we'd expected.

Jess and Angela were going to walk down to the bay. I told them I would meet them at the restaurant in an hour — I wanted to look for a bookstore.

This isn't what I was looking for...

Stay away from me.

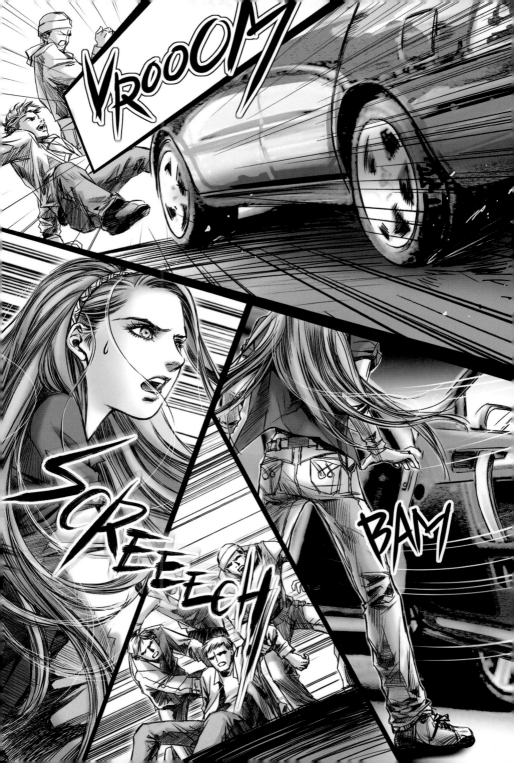

No. He...mentioned your family. And...after that...

...I did some research on the Internet.

Nothing fit. Most of it was kind of silly. And then...

What?

I decided it didn't matter.

It didn't *matter?*

When I went to bed that night, my mind still swirled dizzily, full of images I couldn't understand.

Nothing seemed clear at first, but as I fell gradually closer to unconsciousness, a few certainties became evident.

About three things I was absolutely positive.

First, Edward was a vampire.
Second, there was part of him — and I didn't know how potent that part might be — that thirsted for my blood.
And third,
I was unconditionally and irrevocably in love with him.

Do you want
to ride with me
today?

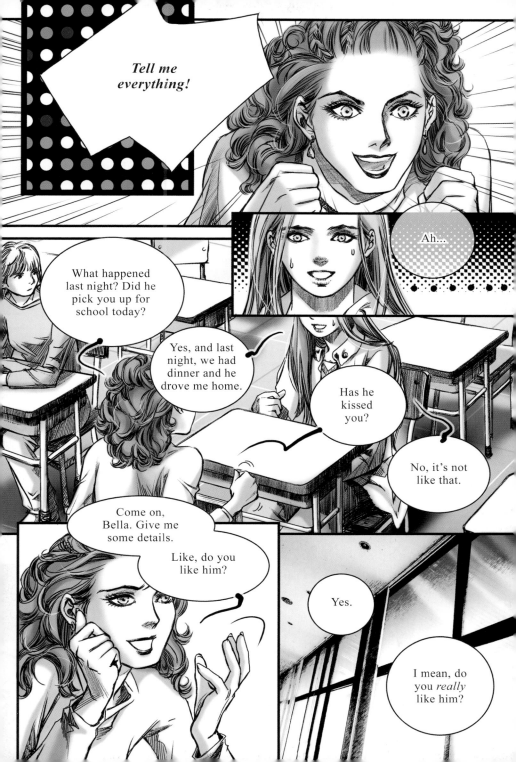

So.

You and Cullen, huh?

That's none of your business, Mike.

I don't like it.

He looks at you like...like you're something to eat.

PFFT

GIGGLE...

?

So how was Gym?

...Are you finished? Is it my turn tomorrow?

Not even close.

What more is there?

You'll find out tomorrow.

CLICK

How late is it?

Another complication,
Edward had said.

Billy stared at me with intense,
anxious eyes. Had Billy recognized
Edward so easily?

Could he really believe the impossible
legends his son had scoffed at?

The answer was clear
in Billy's eyes.

Yes. Yes,
he could.

My mood was blissful the
next morning, and I decided
to forget about the tense
moment with Billy.

When I got outside, Edward
was already waiting for me.

I should have let
you drive yourself
today, since I'm
leaving with Alice
after lunch.

And finally...

...it was Saturday.

KNOCK KNOCK

CLICK

Where are we going?

It's a place I like to go when the weather is nice.

I reached the edge of the pool of light and stepped through the last fringe of ferns...

...into the loveliest place I had ever seen.

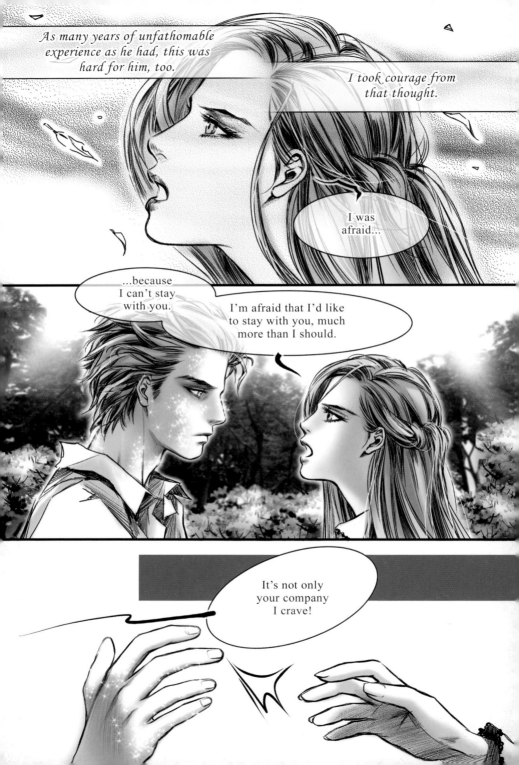

Ah...

It won't
be so hard
again.

...There's something
I wanted to try.

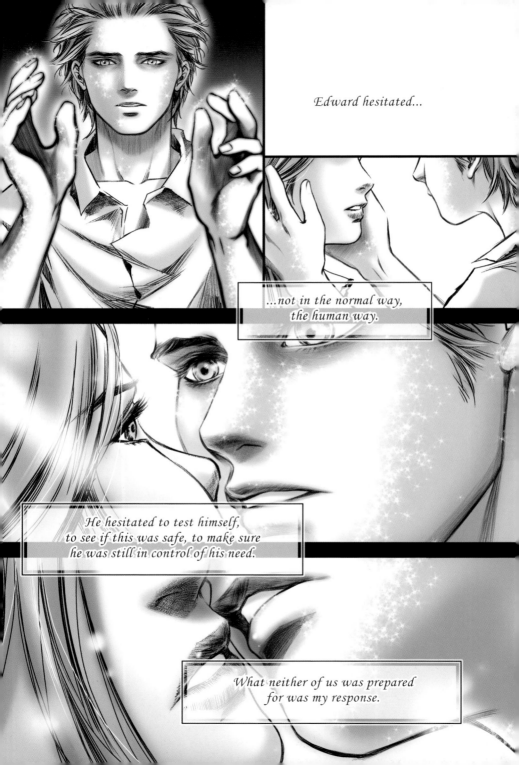

Edward hesitated...

...not in the normal way,
the human way.

He hesitated to test himself,
to see if this was safe, to make sure
he was still in control of his need.

What neither of us was prepared
for was my response.

Before I realized, we were
back at the truck...and by
the time we got back to my
house, the world had turned
quiet and dark...

*To be continued in Volume Two...*